Down by the Cool of the Pool

For George, Harriet, Doris and Guthrie,
and the cool of the pool in France – T.M.

For the lovely chucklesome little Joe – G.P.R.

ORCHARD BOOKS
First published in Great Britain in 2001 by The Watts Publishing Group
This edition first published in 2016
Text © Tony Mitton 2001
Illustrations © Guy Parker Rees 2001
The moral rights of the author and illustrator have been asserted.
All rights reserved.
A CIP catalogue record for this book is available from the British Library.
ISBN 978 1 40834 689 1
Printed and bound in China

Orchard Books
An imprint of Hachette Children's Group
Part of The Watts Publishing Group Limited
Carmelite House
50 Victoria Embankment
London EC4Y 0DZ

An Hachette UK Company
www.hachette.co.uk
www.hachettechildrens.co.uk

Down by the Cool of the Pool

Tony Mitton   **Guy Parker-Rees**

ORCHARD

Duck came to see.
"I can dance too.
But not like you.
I can flap."

Sheep came to see.
"I can dance too.
But not like you.
I can stamp."

So Sheep went

Stamp,

Goat butted in
with a **skip**
and a **hop**,

and Frog cried,
"Wheeeee!
That's great! Don't stop."

Then Playful Pony began to prance

and Donkey drummed his hoofbeat dance,

and a "**flap**" and a

wheeeee!

the animals danced so joyfully,

and a "**Whoops!** Watch out . . . !" and a **topple**", and a . . .

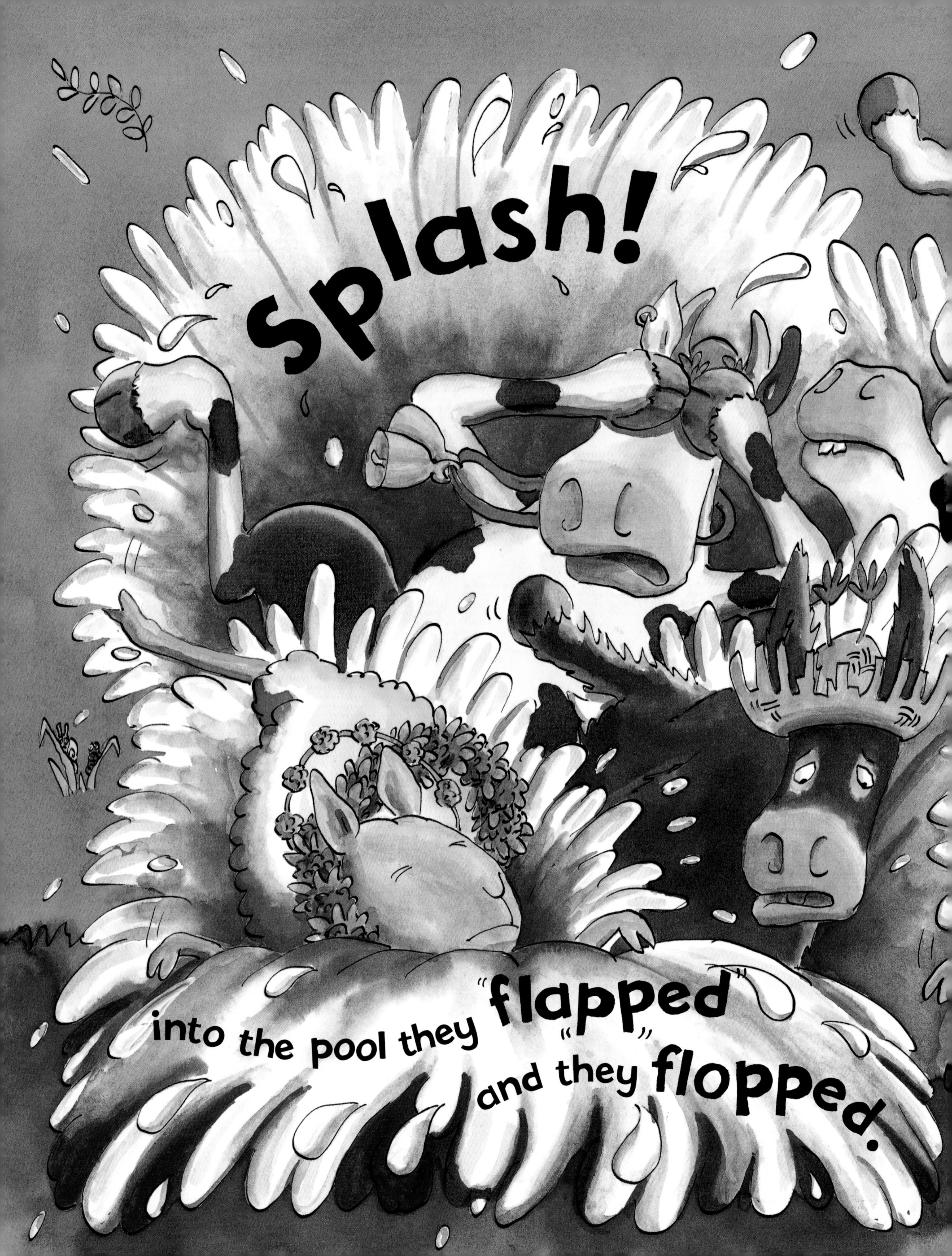

Splash!

into the pool they **flapped**
and they **flopped.**

But did that stop them?

We're having fun, dancing our dance **in** the cool of the pool!"

And they **splished** and **splashed** till their dance was done,

then away they drifted

and down went the sun,

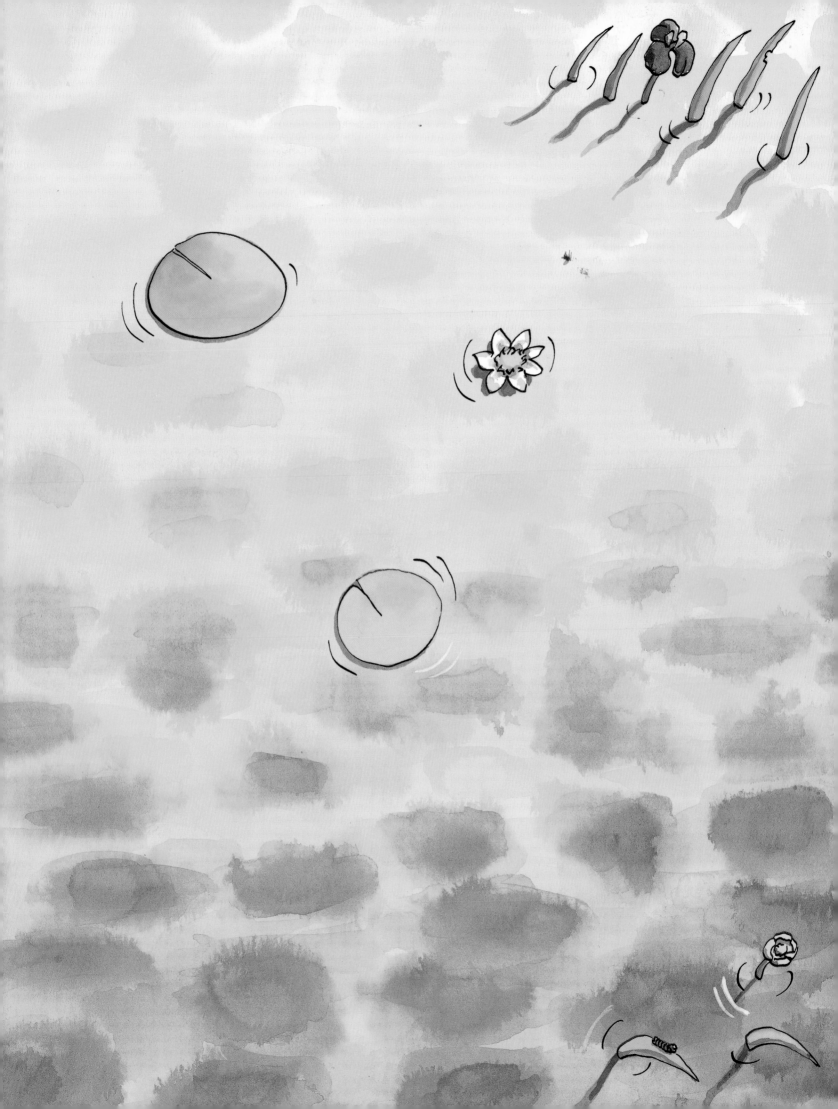